HOLI HAI!

Chitra Soundar

illustrated by

Darshika Varma

Albert Whitman & Company
Chicago, Illinois

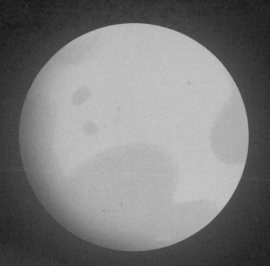

Thank you, Margaret and Mo, for brightening the colors of my writing.

Wishing Isaac and Oscar the color of love forever and ever!—CS

In memory of my loving Maa, who left us on this colourful morning.—DV

Library of Congress Cataloging-in-Publication data is on file with the publisher.
Text copyright © 2022 by Chitra Soundar
Illustrations copyright © 2022 by Albert Whitman & Company • Illustrations by Darshika Varma
First published in the United States of America in 2022 by Albert Whitman & Company
ISBN 978-0-8075-3357-4 (hardcover) • ISBN 978-0-8075-3358-1 (ebook)
Printed in China
10 9 8 7 6 5 4 3 2 1 RRD 26 25 24 23 22 21
Design by Aphelandra
For more information about Albert Whitman & Company, visit our website at www.albertwhitman.com.

The moon was round and almost full.

"Two more sleeps to Holi," said Gauri.

"One and two," counted Aneesh.

The next morning, Grandma held out a bowl full of colored paper. "Gather around! Let's pick gulal to make."

"What is gulal, Grandma?" asked Gauri.

"All the colors we will splash and smear on Holi day," Grandma replied, "to celebrate spring."

"We're going to make them from nature," said Dad.

"From leaves, spices..."

"And flowers," finished Aneesh.

Everyone closed their eyes and pulled out a colored paper from the bowl. Dad had blue. Mom grabbed green. Grandma picked saffron orange. Grandpa had purple. Aneesh got yellow.

Gauri got upset.

"I didn't get my favorite color!" she yelled,
scrunching the paper in her fist. "I don't want red.
I want yellow."

"Gauri, all colors are part of spring," said Mom.
"We keep the colors we picked."

Everyone got busy making gulal. Except Gauri.

Dad boiled cabbage leaves to make blue.
"Want to give me a hand?" he asked.

Gauri shook her head. "No!" she shouted.

Mom spread mint and spinach leaves on the floor to dry. "I'll grind them up to make green," she said. "Would you like to help?"

But Gauri didn't help Mom either.

"Yellow," shouted Aneesh. "With turmeric. Look!"

Grandma rubbed sandalwood on a stone to get saffron orange. "It smells nice," she said.

Grandpa crushed beetroot into a bucket of water.
"This will make a nice purple," he said.

But Gauri didn't join in.

That night, Dad started a bonfire.

Grandpa told them one of the legends of Holi.

"Holika was an evil demoness. But her nephew
Prahlada wasn't evil. He loved everyone and
didn't want to harm anyone. This angered Holika,
and she decided to teach Prahlada a lesson."

"Holika started a blazing fire. 'I'm so evil that the fire can't burn me,' she gloated, extending her arm. 'Come on, nephew. Let's see if your love can save you from the fire's blaze.'"

"Was Prahlada scared?" asked Aneesh.

"Prahlada wasn't scared," said Grandpa. "He wasn't even angry. He knew that love was stronger than his aunt's anger. Prahlada stepped into the fire with Holika."

"Oh no!" said Gauri.

"Don't worry," said Grandpa. "A few minutes later, Prahlada walked out of the fire alone and unharmed. He had shown everyone that love was stronger than evil."

"The fire is like the anger in Holika's heart," said Grandma. "Anger didn't bring her joy."

"When we celebrate Holi tomorrow, we will have love in our hearts for everyone," said Mom, "just like Prahlada did."

Gauri thought about the anger in her heart. Could she let it go and be more like Prahlada?

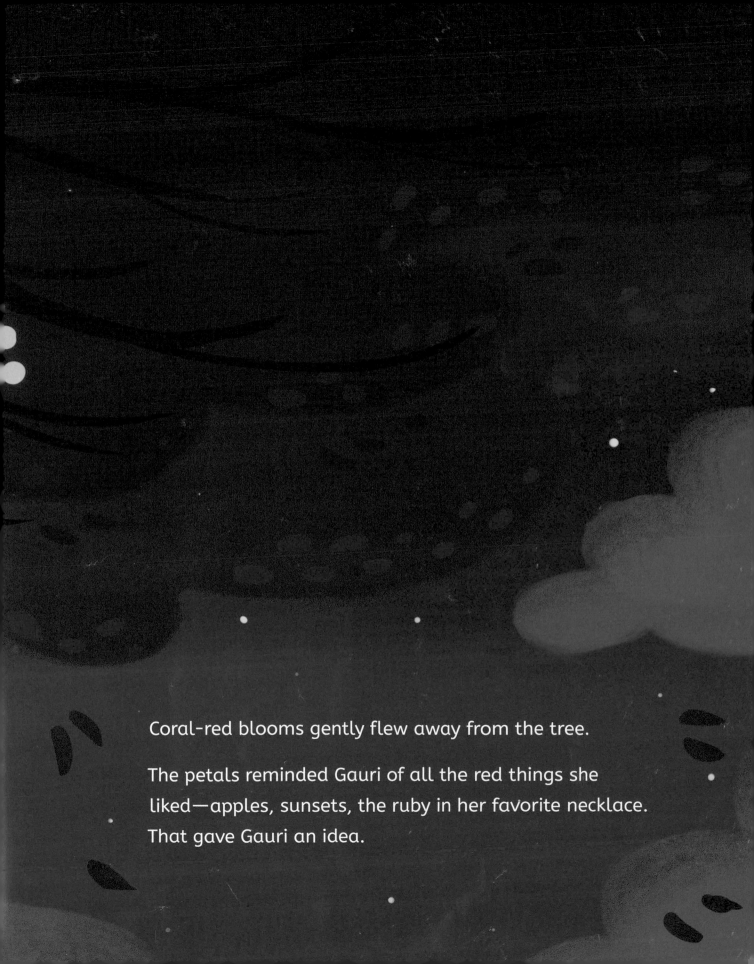

Coral-red blooms gently flew away from the tree.

The petals reminded Gauri of all the red things she
liked—apples, sunsets, the ruby in her favorite necklace.
That gave Gauri an idea.

That evening, while everyone was busy, Gauri gathered the coral-red petals and spread them on a sheet of newspaper. Then she rolled Grandma's stone pestle over them, crushing the petals into powder.

The next morning...

"Red!" cried Aneesh.
"Gauri's gulal."

Grandma pulled Gauri into a hug.
"Red is the color of love," she said.

"And apples and rubies and sunsets,"
said Gauri. "And anger too. I'm sorry
I got upset."

"I forgive your anger with my calming
saffron," said Grandma, spreading
sandalwood paste on Gauri's cheeks.

In the garden, they sprayed and splashed colors at one another—yellow, orange, blue, purple, green, and red.

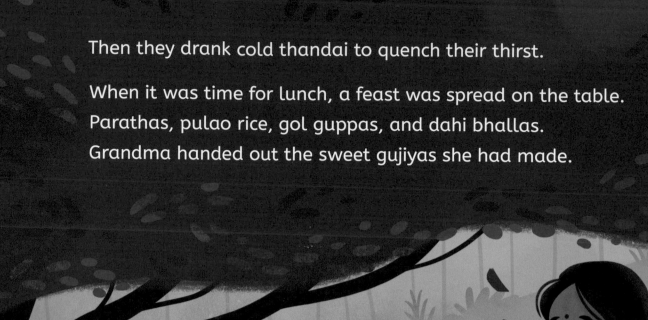

Then they drank cold thandai to quench their thirst.

When it was time for lunch, a feast was spread on the table.
Parathas, pulao rice, gol guppas, and dahi bhallas.
Grandma handed out the sweet gujiyas she had made.

"Today is the first day of spring," said Grandpa.
"Time for new beginnings."

"Today is the day of love," said Grandma.
"All fights are forgotten."

"Holi hai!" called Gauri.

"Holi hai!" wished everyone.

About the Festival

Holi, the festival of colors, is celebrated across India to mark the onset of spring. In the south of India, this festival is celebrated by some communities as the festival of love. There are many origin stories for this festival, one of which, the story of Prahlada, is explained in this book.

The day before Holi, families get together to prepare colors, gather wood for the bonfire, and make delicacies for the main festival. Later that night, they celebrate Choti Holi by lighting the bonfire to mark the defeat of the evil demoness Holika by her young nephew Prahlada.

The morning of the Holi festival is called Rangwali Holi (colorful Holi). Families wake up early, get ready (often in white clothes bought just for the occasion), and play with colors to welcome spring. They spray, smear, and throw colors at one another.

Usually these festivities happen in an open space, to the accompaniment of drumbeats and music that inspires dancing and merrymaking with families, friends, and neighbors. Lunch is served with seasonal produce, bread, rice, and a treat of snacks and street food (as this festival is often celebrated in the streets). In the evening, everyone washes up, changes into clean clothes, and relaxes with their loved ones.

Glossary

coral tree or Erythrina: a type of red flowering tree that grows in warm and temperate coastal cities across the world.

dahi bhalla: a doughball, deep-fried and soaked in yogurt with spicy and tangy toppings.

gol guppa: a round, hollow, deep-fried crepe filled with spicy potatoes and dipped in mint and tamarind water. Often eaten as a snack, it is a popular street food in India.

gujiya: a deep-fried dumpling filled with a mixture of milk solids, raisins with chopped nuts like cashews and almonds.

gulal: the colored powders and liquids made to spray and smear on one another. They are symbols of the colors of spring. The colors are also called abhir.

Holi: a festival celebrated by Hindus worldwide to mark the arrival of spring. It's also called the festival of colors and festival of love.

Holi hai: a traditional greeting during the celebration of the festival. It means "It's Holi" or "Holi is here."

parathas: Indian flatbreads made from wheat flour called atta. Sometimes they are filled with vegetables or meat.

pulao: rice cooked with raisins and spices like saffron, cardamom, and cloves.

thandai: a cold drink made with almond milk, tea, and spices on Holi day and on other hot summer days.

Make Your Own Gulal from Nature

Want to celebrate Holi at home?
Here are some easy ways to make colored water
for your next Holi celebration.

 **Purple:** Have an adult chop beets into small pieces. Place them in a pan, fill the pan with water, and ask an adult to boil the water. Allow the water to cool. Remove the beets.

 Yellow: Mix two tablespoons of turmeric powder in a bucket of cold water.

 **Red:** Peel one or two pomegranate fruits. Fill a pan with water. With the help of an adult, boil the peels in the water, remove the peels, and let the water cool.

 **Blue:** Fill a pan with water. Place shredded red cabbage leaves into the water, and ask for an adult's help to simmer the water for ten minutes. Strain out the cabbage leaves. The water will be purple. Now add ¼ teaspoon of baking powder. Slowly, the color will change from purple to blue. Allow the water to cool.

 **Green:** Have an adult grind spinach and mint leaves into a paste with some oil. Then mix the paste into a bucketful of cold water.

Remember to celebrate safely.